A PICTURE BOOK STUDIO **LITTLE BOOK**

NEUGEBAUER PRESS · LONDON


*an imprint of Neugebauer Press Publishing Ltd., London.*
*Distributed in UK by Ragged Bears, Andover.*
*Distributed in Canada by Vanwell Publishing, St. Catharines, Ont.*
*Distributed in Australia by Era Publications Ltd., Adelaide.*

*Printed in Italy by GIORGIO, Verona.*

*ISBN 1-85618-018-2*

## **LITTLE BOOKS** MY FIRST LIBRARY

*Ask your bookseller for these other LITTLE BOOKS published by Picture Book Studio:*

**1** *THUMBELINA · H.C. Andersen / Lisbeth Zwerger*
**2** *HANSEL AND GRETEL · The Brothers Grimm / Lisbeth Zwerger*
**3** *THE STAR DOLLARS · The Brothers Grimm / Eve Tharlet*
**4** *BESSIE · Peggy Blakeley / Iskender Gider*
**5** *SARAH'S BEAR · Marta Koči*
**6** *HELLO, BEAR! · Achim Bröger / Ivan Gantschev*
**7** *LITTLE RED CAP · The Brothers Grimm / Lisbeth Zwerger*
**8** *THE SWINEHERD · H.C. Andersen / Lisbeth Zwerger*
**9** *THE BREMEN TOWN MUSICIANS · Grimm / Josef Paleček*
**10** *THE THREE LITTLE PIGS · Alan Marks*
**11** *THE SEVEN RAVENS · The Brothers Grimm / Lisbeth Zwerger*
**12** *DIZZY FROM FOOLS · M. L. Miller / Eve Tharlet*
**13** *MACRIBBECK OF RIBBECK · Theodor Fontane / Marta Koči*
**14** *NOAH & THE ARK & THE ANIMALS · Clements / Gantschev*
**15** *PETER AND THE WOLF · Sergei Prokofiev / Josef Paleček*
**16** *JACK IN LUCK · The Brothers Grimm / Eve Tharlet*
**17** *THE NIGHTINGALE · H. C. Andersen / Lisbeth Zwerger*
**18** *MOTHER HOLLE · The Brothers Grimm / Kirsten Höcker*
**19** *LITTLE NERINO · Helga Galler*
**20** *THE PRINCESS AND THE PEA · H. C. Andersen / Eve Tharlet*
**21** *THE WISHING TABLE · The Brothers Grimm / Eve Tharlet*
**22** *KATIE'S KITTEN · Marta Koči*
**23** *MY BIRTHDAY BOOK · Ivan Gantschev*
**24** *SIMON AND THE HOLY NIGHT · Eve Tharlet*

*More LITTLE BOOKS to follow!*

# Mother Holle

*by the Brothers Grimm*

*illustrated by Kirsten Höcker*

*translated from the German by Anthea Bell*

Once upon a time there was a widow who had two daughters. One of them was a pretty, hard-working girl, but the other was ugly and lazy. However, the widow loved the ugly, lazy girl, who was her own daughter, much more than the other. So the hardworking girl, her stepdaughter, had to do all the work about the place and was the household drudge.

Every day she had to sit by a well and spin until her fingers were bleeding.

Now it happened that one day her bobbin was covered
with blood. The girl leaned over the well to wash it,
but as she did so the bobbin slipped out of her hand
and fell down the well. Weeping, she ran to her stepmother
and told her about this misfortune. Her stepmother was
very cross, and said, "You let the bobbin fall down the well,
so you can fetch it out again!"
The girl did not know what to do.
She went back to the well,
and in her despair she jumped right into it.

She lost consciousness, and when she woke and came back to her senses she found herself in a meadow. The sun was shining, and the air was sweet with the scent of flowers. She walked on across this meadow, and came to an oven full of bread.

"Oh, take me out, take me out, or I'll burn!" cried the bread. "I'm done to a turn!"

So the girl went up to the oven and took the bread out with a wooden shovel.

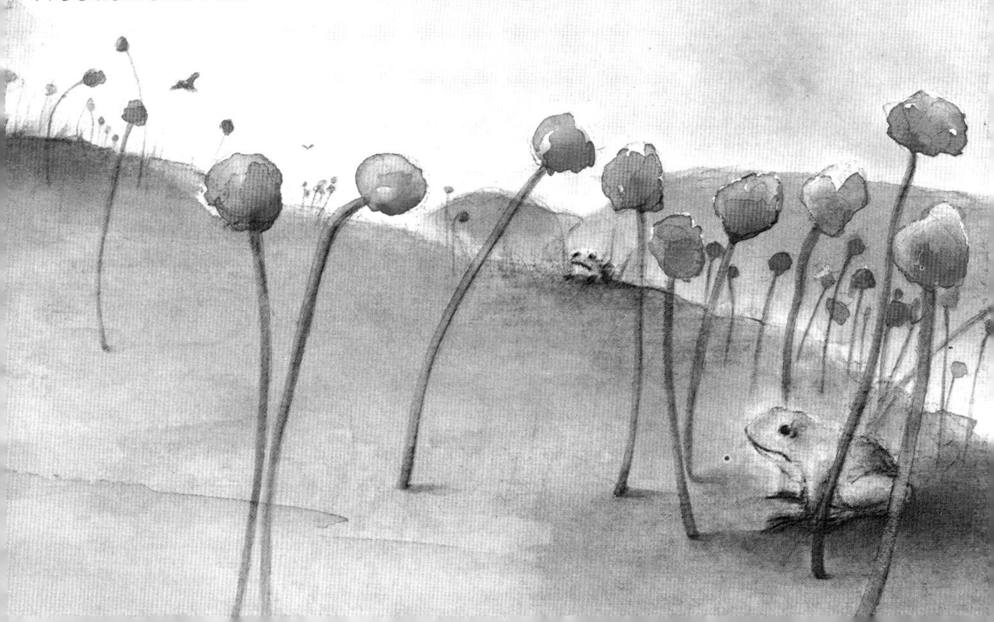

Then she went on, and came to a tree laden with apples. "Oh, shake me, shake me!" cried the apple tree. "My apples are all ripe." So the girl shook the apple tree, and the apples tumbled to the ground. She shook it until there was not an apple left on the tree, and when she had gathered the apples into a heap she went on again.

At last she came to a little house, and saw an old woman with big teeth looking out of the window. The girl was very scared, and turned to run away, but the old woman called, "What are you afraid of, my child? Stay here with me. If you do the housework properly all will be well with you. Above all, you must shake my bed well every day until the feathers fly, because that is when it snows on earth. For I am Mother Holle."

The old woman spoke so kindly that the girl plucked up her courage, and she went to work as Mother Holle's maidservant.

The girl did everything to the old woman's satisfaction. She shook Mother Holle's bed so hard that the feathers flew through the air like snowflakes, and then it snowed on earth. She was very comfortable with the old woman, who gave her a delicious meal every day and never a cross word. However, when she had been there a long time she began to feel sad. At first she did not know what the matter was, but then she realized that she was homesick. Although Mother Holle had treated her so well she wanted to go home, but it was some time before she dared say so. "Well," said Mother Holle, "I am glad that you love your home, comfortable as you were with me, and since you have served me so faithfully I will take you back to earth myself."

Taking the girl by the hand, she led her to a great gate.
ıen it opened, and just as the girl was standing in the gateway,
a great shower of gold fell on her. The gold clung so that she
vas covered all over with it. "The gold is for you, because you
ıve served me faithfully," said Mother Holle, and she also gave
her back the bobbin that had fallen down the well.

Then she closed the gate, and the girl found herself up on earth again, quite near her stepmother's house. As she walked into the yard the rooster on the rim of the well crowed

*"Cock-a-doodle-do, cock-a-doodle-do,*
*Our golden girl is home again, cock-a-doodle-do!"*

Then she hurried to her stepmother and her sister, and they welcomed her kindly, because she was covered with gold.

She told them her story, and when the stepmother heard how one of the girls had come by such riches, she wanted the other to have the same good fortune. So the ugly, lazy daughter had to sit by the well and spin. She pricked her finger and scratched her hand on the thorn hedge to make her bobbin bloody, and then she threw it down the well and jumped in after it.

Like the hard-working girl, the lazy one found herself in the meadow, and walked the same way until she came to the oven. "Oh, take me out, take me out, or I'll burn!" cried the bread. "I'm done to a turn." But the lazy girl said, "I don't want to get all dirty!" and walked on. Soon she came to the apple tree. "Oh, shake me, shake me!" cried the tree. "My apples are all ripe." But she said, "What an idea! Suppose an apple fell on my head?" And she walked on.

When she came to Mother Holle's house she was not afraid, because she had heard about the old woman's big teeth, and she took service with her at once. On the first day she forced herself to work hard and did everything Mother Holle told her. But she kept thinking of all the gold she would get as her wages.

Next day, however, she began idling, and the day after that she wouldn't even get up in the morning.
She did not make Mother Holle's bed or shake it till the feather flew. Mother Holle had soon had enough of her, and told her to leave.
The lazy girl was glad of that, thinking that now she would g the shower of gold.

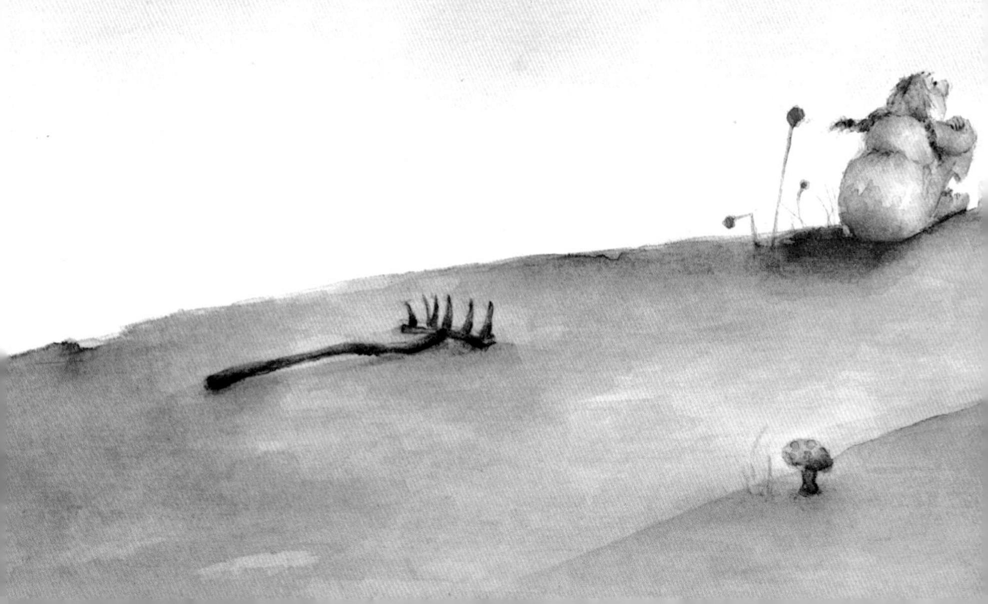

Mother Holle led her to the gate in her turn, but as the lazy girl stood in the gateway a shower not of gold but of pitch fell on her. "That's the wages I owe you for your services," said Mother Holle, shutting the gate.

So the lazy girl went home, all covered with pitch.

When rooster standing on the rim of the well saw the girl, he crowed:

*"Cock-a-doodle-doo, cock-a-doodle-do,*
*Our dirty girl is home again, cock-a-doodle-do!"*

And the pitch stuck so fast to her that she could never get it off as long as she lived.